James Baker

Slavery

James Baker

Slavery

ISBN/EAN: 9783337398378

Printed in Europe, USA, Canada, Australia, Japan

Cover: Foto ©Andreas Hilbeck / pixelio.de

More available books at **www.hansebooks.com**

SLAVERY:

BY

J. L. BAKER.

AUTHOR OF "EXPORTS AND IMPORTS," "MEN AND THINGS," &c.

———

PHILADELPHIA:

JOHN A. NORTON,

1860.

SLAVERY.

THE recent attempt of John Brown to incite an insurrection at Harper's Ferry has created no little excitement throughout the country. Strange and desperate as the movement was, it seems to have been the natural and necessary result of the long twenty years' war, waged in the free States upon the institutions of the South, the culminating point, it is to be hoped, in a reform based on no sound principle, and which, like an epidemic, has swept over the land, fruitful only in bitter words, harsh recrimination, sectional hostility, and ending, like the last act of a tragedy, in violence and murder.

The scene that has been enacted at Harper's Ferry will perhaps have the effect to open the eyes of the nation, so that they can see fully the yawning gulf, the brink of which they have at last reached, and lead them to examine the ground on which they stand ; inquire what they have been doing, and what good cause can be served by a course of action which has led to such fatal results. Many lives have been sacrificed. A whole family has been ruined, and an old man has been led out to suffer the last and most terrible infliction of the law. He has been but an instrument in the hands of others, who have acted, with the exception of some political leaders, from honest convictions.

The time has now come, however, for them to inquire, and for all to inquire with the utmost seriousness, if these convictions of duty have been just and commendable, or if they have been mistaken, and therefore to be condemned. Zeal without knowledge is a dangerous weapon, as all history has proved, and it is incumbent upon all, not only to do right, but to think right. It is an old maxim that ignorance of the law excuses no man, and it is equally true that we are not at liberty to follow our blind impulses, but are bound to inform ourselves, and to know whether a particular course of action, however well intended, is such as will not defeat the very purposes we have in view, while it brings misery and ruin to thousands of our fellow beings.

Liberty has been in all ages of the world a most fruitful theme for the poet and the orator, and still its true nature and conditions are but imperfectly understood. Constitutional liberty, such as that of England and the United States, is possible only to a race that has a physical temperament that fits it for self-control or self-government, and to such a race only is it a blessing. But few such races have been known in history. One of them was the Grecian, and afterwards the Roman, but both became degenerated, and lost the capacity of self-government.

In modern times the English nation has exhibited the same capacity, which belongs also to ourselves, who are of the same blood. No other people have those constitutional traits which fit them for self-government, which is but another name for self-restraint. The Frenchman is volatile, fickle, and fond of glory, and less free to-day than he was under Louis the Sixteenth. He has a government which answers to his wants and his genius, which exactly represents his condition, and contributes, therefore, most to his happiness. Should he, in the course of centuries, become changed in his physical and mental constitution, he will find, necessarily, a government that corresponds to the progress he has made. Governments are but the agents and representatives of the people. They reflect very nearly the condition of the governed, and change to meet the changes of those they represent. No mortal power can prevent any people from taking and enjoying that degree of freedom they are capable of enjoying, and which would, therefore, contribute to their happiness. What is true of France, is true of the other European nations, and of all nations; so that we never deceive ourselves more completely than when we talk of political liberty as something equally applicable to all, and attainable by all.

Such liberty the Anglo-Saxon finds contributing to his happiness; but it may be the greatest curse, as it has often proved to those who have different blood in their veins, who have not the same capacity of self-control, and who enjoy, therefore, as much, if not more, under governments suited to their peculiar temperaments. An Italian Republic exists only in the dreams of Mazzini and Garibaldi, and yet if the sum of human happiness could be measured, there may be as much happiness in Italy, and perhaps more than is to be found in the two nations that are able to live under a constitutional government.

It often happens, that among those nations which require a strong government, we find a larger amount of social freedom, than among those who are politically more free. A man is more free to express an opinion in Paris, upon any matter of science or religion, or other topic, excepting politics, than he is in Boston. He stands less in awe of his neighbors, feels less the pressure of public opinion, than do we, on whom government bears lightly, but who are, to a corresponding extent, the slaves of Public Sentiment. Where laws bear lightest, Public Opinion takes their place, and becomes, often, a dreadful tyrant, as is seen frequently in our western States, and on the borders of civilization. On the other hand, where there exists the least political freedom, we find the largest social liberty, as though one was incompatible with the other, which is probably the case, and for the reason that man must be governed to a certain extent in some way, and if he becomes politically more free, he becomes by necessity, socially, more enslaved.

We shall find, if we look at the different nations of the world, that each enjoys that degree of liberty, either political or social, which most contributes to its happiness. If this were not the case with any nation, it is certain that its condition would be changed at once, to correspond to its wants and capacities. No government, however despotic, could for a moment prevent such a result; nor is it at all safe to judge of the real condition of a nation, by the ex-cited harangues of such enthusiasts as Kossuth and Mazzini.

As fast as a people become capable of self-control or self-govern-ment, just so fast the government becomes modified to meet their wants; for they are in fact the government, and rulers are but their representatives.

This view of liberty will be considered, I am aware, by many as very heretical and not at all in accordance with the facts of history or the nature of man. To some it will, no doubt, appear new as well as strange, and very doubtful. That what we call constitutional liberty, however, depends mainly upon the pe-culiar physical and moral temperament of a people, I cannot doubt. Self-government is constitutional in more senses than one. Such at least is the result of my reflections upon the subject. The lesson I learn from history is, that no amount of physical or mental culture can materially change the peculiar temperament which belongs to each race. A nation may be educated to excel in all the arts and all the sciences, in oratory, philosophy, poetry, music, and painting, but not in the art of self-government, which implies a natural gift bestowed upon a very small portion of the human race. To judge of a people in this respect we must also witness their capacity at home, and not be deceived by what happens to individuals or small communities when thrown into the midst of a self-controlling or self-governing race. Such is the case with our German population which constitutes an intelligent, useful, law-abiding portion of our citizens, and to all appearance capable of exercising the functions of self-government. But we must consider that they exist here surrounded and entirely controlled by our own people, and in some parts of the Union have been born and brought up under our institutions. If we wish to know the capacity of their race for self-government, we must go to Germany, and if possible find it there. The German race comes nearest to our own and excels it in some respects, though wanting the necessary political elements with which we are gifted. For many years the profoundest scholars and the greatest musical composers have been found in Germany, which has also produced in Gœthe and Schiller, names worthy to rank with the greatest of modern times. We come from the same stock and the same northern hive, but have pursued different courses, and have not now the same blood in our veins. One race takes naturally to politics, for which it has an aptitude and capacity, the other as naturally to music and painting, to science and philosophy. In the lapse of centuries, the physical constitution of both may change. The English may lose by admixture the peculiar qualities of blood which now distinguish them, and so lose their capacity of self-control. They may become degenerated, like the Romans, by the enervating influence of luxury, and like that nation lose their constitutional liberty. So on the other hand, Germany may, in the progress of time, undergo changes equally great and. in precisely the opposite direction. A union of the different races of that vast kingdom may produce a new result. A new race may arise which shall excel the present race of Englishmen, in the capacity of self-government. The present English race is the work of centuries, and contains the blood of Saxons, Danes, and Normans, blended in due proportion for the production of a certain result, and such a result as can nowhere else be witnessed.

If the theory of human liberty, which I have thus so briefly and imperfectly suggested, is the true one, and is supported by the facts of history, then it will furnish us with a key to unlock some of those hard problems in human life and destiny which have so puzzled mankind, and which have resisted all attempts at solution.

If we regard all nations as moving on in the sphere designed by Providence, each seeking and finding its happiness in its own way,

— some less capable of self-restraint than others, some enjoying a high degree of political liberty, and some, on the other hand, in possession of a high degree of social freedom; their happiness dependent not so much on the peculiar forms of their government as upon its adaptation to their peculiar wants and capacities,—we shall be relieved of much of that commiseration and misplaced sympathy which we have bestowed upon others, and which was, perhaps, more needed by ourselves. Viewed in the light I have suggested, and also in connection with the great facts, moral and physical, of which I am about to speak more particularly, the problem of negro slavery in the United States is not one so difficult of solution as has been generally supposed. The recent outbreak in Virginia brings home to us, with renewed and redoubled force, the question, What must become of the millions of slaves in our Southern States, could they be set free by some such movement as that of John Brown, urged on by those who have been for many years engaged in agitating the subject?

This is the important matter for our consideration, or rather it should have been the matter to have been considered many years ago. This is the problem which should have been solved by those who have been so long dealing in such extravagant language and "glittering generalities" about the natural rights of man. They should have informed us what is to become of those millions, suddenly let loose from restraint aud thrown upon their own resources, no longer to be protected by the white race, but to be met by competition, by undying prejudice, extreme social hardship, and the "irrepressible conflict" of incompatible races.

Those of us who have attained to middle age have been taught by experience that no portion of those millions could exist for any length of time on the soil of Massachusetts. But for the occasional emigration from the South, a negro would now be a sight as rare in this State as that of a wild Indian, hardly a remnant being left of the families which we knew in our boyhood.

From statistics gathered by the late Dr. Jesse Chickering, it appears that the blacks die in Massachusetts in a ratio of three to one as compared with the whites. This state of things is the result of both moral and physical causes. The depressing influence of extreme social hardship, which no philanthropy can alleviate, accounts in a great measure for this unequal mortality; while physical causes operate, perhaps, still more to the same effect. Of the latter, we may learn something from a paper read a few years since before the Boston Society of Natural History, by Dr. Samuel Kneeland, Jr., from which the following is an extract: —

"The mulatto is often triumphantly appealed to as a proof that hybrid races are prolific without end. Every physician who has seen much practice among the mulattoes knows that, in the first place, they are far less prolific than the blacks or whites,—the statistics of New York State and city confirm this fact of daily observation ; and, in the second place, when they are prolific, the progeny is frail, diseased, short-lived, rarely arriving at robust manhood or maturity. Physicians need not be told of the comparatively enormous amount of scrofulous and deteriorated constitutions found among those hybrids.

"The Colonization Journal furnishes some statistics with regard to the colored population of New York city, which must prove painfully interesting to all reflecting people. The late census showed that, while other classes of our population in all parts of the country were increasing in an enormous ratio, the colored were decreasing. In the State of New York, in 1840, there were fifty thousand; in 1850, only forty-seven thousand. In New York city, in 1840, there were eighteen thousand ; in 1850, seventeen thousand. According to the New York City Inspector's report for the four months, ending with October, 1853 : —

1. The whites present marriages, ... 2,230
   The colored   "   "   26
2. The whites   "   births, ... 6,780
   The colored   "   "   70
3. The whites   "   deaths about   6,000
      (exclusive of 2,152 among 116,000 newly-arrived
         emigrants, and others unacclimated.)
   The colored exhibit deaths, ... 160

giving a ratio of deaths among acclimated whites to colored persons of thirty-seven to one; while the births are ninety-seven whites to one colored. The ratio of whites to colored, is as follows : — Marriages, 140 to 1 ; births, 97 to 1 ; deaths, 37 to 1. According to the ratio of the population, the marriages among the whites, during this time, are three times greater than among the colored ; the number of births among the whites is twice as great. In deaths, the colored exceed the white not only according to ratio of population, but show one hundred and sixty-five deaths to seventy-six births, or seven deaths to three births,—more than two to one.

"The same is true of Boston, as far as the census returns will enable us to judge. In Shattuck's census of 1845, it appears that in that year there were one hundred and forty-six less colored persons in Boston than in 1840; the total number being 1842. From the same work, the deaths are given for a period of fifty years, from 1725 to 1775, showing the mortality among the blacks to have been twice that among the whites. Of late years, Boston, probably, does not differ from itself in former times, nor from New York at present. In the compendium of the United States census for 1850, p. 64, it is said that the 'declining ratio of the increase of the free colored in every section is notable. In New England, the increase is now almost nothing;' in the south-west and the Southern states, the increase is much reduced; it is only in the north-west that there is any increase, 'indicating a large emigration to that quarter.' What must become of the black population at this rate in a few years? What are the causes of this decay? They do not disregard the laws of social and physical well-being any more than, if they do as much as, the whites. It seems to me one of the necessary consequences of attempts to mix races; the hybrids cease to be prolific; the race must die out as mulatto; it must either keep black unmixed, or become extinct. Nobody doubts that a mixed offspring may be produced by intermarriage of different races, — the Griquas, the Papuas, the Cafuses of Brazil, so elaborately enumerated by Prichard, sufficiently prove this. The question is, whether they would be perpetuated if strictly confined to intermarriage among themselves? From the facts in the case of mulattoes, we say unquestionably not. The same is true, as far as has been observed, of the mixture of the white and red races, in Mexico, Central and South America. The well-known infrequency of mixed offspring between the European and Australian races, led the Colonial government to official inquiries, and to the result, that, in thirty-one districts, numbering fifteen thousand inhabitants, the half-breeds did not exceed two hundred, though the connection of the two races was very intimate.

"If any one wishes to be convinced of the inferiority and tendency to disease in the mulatto race, even with the assistance of the pure blood of the black and white race, he need only witness what I did recently, viz.: the disembarkation from a steamboat of a colored pic-nic party, of both sexes, of all ages, from the infant in arms to the aged, and of all hues, from the darkest black to a color approaching white. There was no *old mulatto*, though there were several *old negroes*; many fine-looking mulattoes of both sexes, evidently the first offspring from the pure races; then came the youths and children, and here could be read the sad truth at a glance. The little blacks were agile and healthy-looking; the little mulattoes, youths and young women, farther removed from the pure stocks, were sickly, feeble, thin, with frightful scars and skin diseases, and *scrofula* stamped on every feature and every visible part of the body. Here was hybridity of human races, under the most favorable circumstances of worldly condition and social position."

Such are the results of an unfavorable climate and the mixture of the blood of two races that can never intermarry. The union of such races produces the results described by Dr. Kneeland. Similar results are observed when the two races differ less and where marriage is possible, as for instance in Mexico and Central America, which are in ruins from the union of the Spanish and native blood. Union of different races is, on the other hand, often highly beneficial, our own blood being a fortunate result of such a union, but such races must be similar and not like those of Europe, Africa, and the natives of this country, wholly dissimilar or repugnant. At the South, the free black would suffer less from the effects of climate; but much more from the extreme prejudice existing there towards the black, when he assumes the position of an equal. To suppose he could exist under such a state of things is to ignore all experience, and the observation of every day. In Jamaica, the English Government have troops to protect the freed slaves from the encroachments of their old masters; but there it is stated, on the authority of the London Times, that the blacks are not only falling below the point of civilization attained during their servitude, but in many cases actually returning to their native barbarism, and the worship of idols. We have no such standing army here, but the slave, when free, must be left to the tender mercies of his former master. What would be the fate of the slave is as certain as is the fate of the North American Indian, the difference being that the Indian flies from civilization, which destroys him, while the imitative and mild-tempered African clings to civilization which as certainly destroys *him*. How far he may rise in the scale of civilization if left to himself, whether the African is a self-sustaining and progressive race, or whether it will lose, when left to itself, what has been gained, and fall back in a state of barbarism, are questions not settled as yet by experiment. The attempt is making in Liberia, and it is to be hoped successfully, to solve this question in favor of the negro; but sufficient time has not yet elapsed, nor is the testimony which comes from the West Indies by any means such as could be wished.

From some of our Western States the colored man has been entirely excluded. This is a wise provision, and a merciful one, to the blacks, who come into the free States only to drag out a few years in some menial employment, and then disappear with their families, if they have any, leaving no trace behind. If history and experience teach us anything, it is this, that two races constituted like the Anglo-Saxon and the African, can never co-exist in a state of equality, which means competition. So long as the inferior race is in a dependent condition, and can claim support and protection from the white, it remains, with rare exceptions, contented and happy, the great burden of such a relation falling, in fact, upon the master, and not upon the slave. The moment that relation is changed, the negro thrown upon his own resources, and exposed to the withering and blasting effects of that ineradicable antipathy which exists towards all of African descent, that moment his fate is sealed; he perishes like the autumn leaves when comes a killing frost, and, in course of a very few generations, not a vestige remains to show that he has ever existed.

This is a truth which experience and observation have taught us, and which could not have been taught in the same manner to Mr. Jefferson, and other founders of our government, whose opinions are quoted in favor of the abolition of slavery. That slavery was an evil, they knew, and we know it also, but that the evil is mainly to the white, and that the black could never co-exist with his master in a state of freedom, they did not know, because the experiment had not been tried. Sufficient time has now elapsed to settle that question, and in a manner which would seem to leave but small chance for doubt to a rational mind.

Such, I suppose, to be the immutable law of Providence, regulating the intercourse of those races which he has made, and given to one a white skin, and to the other a dark one. The Creator of all things could, doubtless, have made all white, or all black, but, for some purpose which we cannot fathom, he has chosen not to do so. He has created some races near akin to each other, and some entirely incompatible and repugnant, and it is not for us to say that he has done wrong. If possible, we should ascertain what are the laws, physical and moral, which *he has established*, and then we shall do well to acquiesce in them as being right, without attempting to repeal or improve upon them, or to set up in opposition our own notions about what we call *abstract right*. Right is not an abstraction, but a reality, and, to find out what it is, we have to consult our experience, observation, revelation, expediency, divine laws and human laws, and every source from which we can gather the means of directing our limited capacities to the formation of just conclusions.*

Some may say, perhaps, better let them perish then, than remain in slavery. As the slaves do not say so themselves, I do not, for one, feel warranted in saying it for them. They may, in the designs of Providence, have an important mission to perform,— that mission being, for aught we know, to carry back from their long sojourn in a land of bondage the seeds of civilization to benighted Africa, the home of their fathers. Whatever may be their ultimate fate, I do not feel warranted in hastening and deciding it by exterminating them, or, in other words, dissolving the tie that binds them to those whose duty and interest it is to protect them. A heavy burden lies upon the backs of the masters, which they cannot throw off at will, and with which we are not burdened. They have a sad and perplexing duty to perform, and why should we, by our interference, increase those burdens which we can do nothing to lighten? All such interference is a positive injury to the slave, and insulting to those with whom we have formed a copartnership, and with whom we must live as one family, so long as we continue to be a free people.

One who has a true respect for the colored man and a just regard for his interests, will not, I think, wish to see him placed in a false position, such as he occupies in the free States, hanging for a short time upon the skirts of a community which disowns him, and then sinking into the grave leaving no trace behind. For the negro there is, socially, no hope in the free States, and those who flatter him with such a prospect do him a most grievous wrong. A few of partly African descent and possessed of considerable intellectual endowments have been thus deceived, as they will no doubt have occasion to realize most fully.

As lovers of their race how can they wish to see it occupy its present position in the free States? If they would improve its condition, why not lead out a colony to its native land, where it can live and not die, where it can be relieved from the destroying influence of the Anglo-Saxon, and stand up on its own

---

* Our English common law is said to be the perfection of human wisdom. It is founded in right, and its object is to ascertain and establish the right. The sources from which it is drawn have been thus enumerated. "The law of nature; the revealed law of God; Christianity, morality, and religion; common sense, legal reason, justice, natural equity, humanity."

ground, conscious of no superior, feeling its own dignity, and with ample opportunity for the development of all the faculties with which it has been endowed. Such a work would be worthy of the best intellect and the highest powers that have been bestowed on either black or white; but those of the colored race who are content with delivering anti-slavery lectures, or writing for anti-slavery papers, so far from elevating their race are engaged in a work which can end only in ruin, to the blacks certainly, in the loss of life and entire extinction, and to the whites in the loss it may be of a Union which no art can restore to its original beauty and perfection when once destroyed. As the true friend of the negro, I would not flatter him with delusive hopes and false expectations that can never be realized as has been too often and constantly done by very excellent men, and with the very best intentions; but, I would endeavor, as far as possible, to tell him the truth, however unpalatable, in the full belief that in the end such truth will operate for the best interest of all, black and white, bond and free.

The diversities and repulsions of race which have been ordained, no doubt, for some wise purpose, are intended, perhaps, only for this state of existence. Another life may present a new order of things in which no such distinctions exist. Men have been created to differ from each other physically, morally, and intellectually, but still all are equal before the Creator of all, entitled to an equal share in his bounty, and to the enjoyments of life best suited to the genius and capacity of each. In another world the genius and capacity of all may be alike, all finding happiness in the society of all — and in a mutual pursuit of the same objects, whether of knowledge or of taste, of study or of worship.

It is much to be hoped that this subject will ere long be treated in a very different manner from what it has been for the last fifteen or twenty years. It is simply a question of races, and all the violent and bitter harangues that have been uttered have advanced not one step towards ameliorating the condition of the slave, or solving the problem of negro slavery in this country. Such harangues have only served to stir up strife and jealousy, to set one portion of the people against another portion, array in opposition members of the same family, and finally, when acting upon such fiery spirits and undisciplined minds as that of John Brown, to bring us to the brink of civil and servile war.

In offering the above suggestions, it may be proper to say, that I have done so with entire respect for the personal character and motives of many of those who have been prominent in promoting and bringing upon us the present state of things. I have the best reason to know that some of them have acted from a high sense of duty, and such no doubt is the case with those colored men to whom I have referred. I yield to no one in my regard and sympathy for the colored man, wherever he may be found, and would therefore see him placed in a true position, not in a false and impossible one.

Those who have been so long agitating this subject, however honestly, may still have done so under a mistaken sense of duty, and the time has now come when the subject should be viewed in every aspect and in all its relations, so that, if possible, we can know the ground whereon we stand. No attempt, however humble, to throw light on a subject of such momentous importance should be discouraged, and I cannot therefore feel that any apology is due from me for laying before the community some considerations which may present the subject, to many, in a somewhat new light. If it is true that the two races can never co-exist, in a state of freedom, it is a truth of the utmost importance, and should, therefore, be fully known and understood by all.* If that proposition is not true, its fallacy can no doubt be shown, or at any rate demonstrated by the lapse of time. In my judgment, time has, thus far, proved and confirmed it. The reader will judge from his own experience and observation, and the evidence here presented, how far my conclusion is a just and reasonable one.

When we consider that the slave is supported from birth until he can labor, and from the time when he can no longer work until he dies, and also that at best his services are not worth more than one-third as much as those of free labor, it is very easy to see that he is the best paid laborer in the world, as it is certainly true that a more happy and contented laboring population is not to be found among civilized or uncivilized nations. With rare exceptions, the relation of master and slave in our Southern States is a very happy one, at least to the slave. Kindness and indulgence are the rule, while cruelty and harsh treatment are the exception. Our Northern patience would no doubt soon be exhausted, were we compelled to deal with and provide for a similar class of laborers.

---

* Since the above was written, I find that the same theory is advanced by Mr. Buckle, in his History of Civilization, a very obvious theory, it would seem, and the result of the most common observation, viz : that where two distinct races come together there can be no amalgamation, but the inferior must die out in presence of the superior.

At the same time, the slave is subject to occasional hardships. This is the fate of all, under whatever social system they may live. In some form or other, all men are called on to pay for the privileges they enjoy, nor could it be expected that the slave would be an exception to this general rule. If the marriage bond could be legalized and rendered more sacred, and families not allowed to be separated by sale, many cases of hardship would be prevented. This is a matter for the serious consideration of the slaveholder, if he would manifest to the world a desire to place the dependent race in the best possible condition, consistent with its safety.

Of the possibility of such reforms, they are the best judges, however, who have the burden upon them, and are best acquainted with the wants and capacities of the African race. It is easy for those at a distance to give advice, in regard to a social system, the practical working of which they are quite ignorant of, but those who are born and bred under such system can only know the difficulties that lie in the way of reform, especially when those difficulties are aggravated by interference from abroad.

Slavery may finally come to an end in the United States, by the operation of natural causes, such as the rapid increase and constant encroachment of free labor, and the fact that slave labor is so expensive and tends so greatly to the impoverishing of the soil. As Slavery dies out, the colored race will disappear from the scene forever. It is not for us, I think, to hasten that time by revolution and servile insurrection, to put torches and pikes into the hands of such a population to be used against the whites, in re-enacting all the horrors of a St. Domingo massacre, and at the same time sealing its own fate as suddenly and as rapidly as the dew disappears before the rising sun.

Public sentiment has undergone a marked change in England, on the subject of Slavery, within the last few years. The Anti-Slavery sentiment, like an epidemic, swept over the whole length and breadth of Great Britain, and in its course swept away Slavery in the British West Indies. The natural and inevitable re-action has already taken place in England, and happy will it be for us if it comes in this country before it is too late. That such a re-action is already taking place in the United States, hastened by the foray of John Brown, there is great reason to believe.

The following extracts from the London Times are very significant: —

Effect of Emancipation on the African Race. — There is no blinking the truth. Years of bitter experience; years of hope deferred; of self-devotion unrequited ; of poverty; of humiliation ; of prayers unanswered ; of sufferings derided ; of insults unresented ; of contumely patiently endured,— have convinced us of the truth. It must be spoken out loudly and energetically, despite the wild mockings of "howling cant." The freed West India slave will not till the soil for wages ; the free son of the ex-slave is as obstinate as his sire. He will not cultivate lands which he has not bought for his own. Yams, mangoes, and plantains — these satisfy his wants; he cares not for yours. Cotton, sugar and coffee, and tobacco — he cares but little for them. And what matters it to him that the Englishman has sunk his thousands and tens of thousands on mills, machinery and plants, which now totter on the languishing estate that for years has only returned beggary and debt. He eats his yams, and sniggers at "Buckra."

We know not why this should be, but it is so. The negro has been bought with a price — the price of English taxation and English toil. He has been redeemed from bondage by the sweat and travail of some millions of hard-working Englishmen. Twenty millions of pounds sterling — one hundred millions of dollars — have been distilled from the brains and muscles of the free English laborer, of every degree, to fashion the West Indian negro into a "free and independent laborer." "Free and independent" enough he has become, God knows ; but laborer he is not ; and, so far as we can see, never will be. He will sing hymns and quote texts; but honest, steady industry he not only detests but despises. We wish to Heaven that some people in England — neither Government people nor parsons nor clergymen, but some just-minded, honest-hearted and clearsighted men — would go out to some of the islands (say Jamaica, Dominica, or Antigua) — not for a month or three months, but for a year — would watch the precious *protege* of English philanthropy, the freed negro, in his daily habits; would watch him as he lazily plants his little squatting; would see him as he proudly rejects agricultural or domestic services, or accepts it only at wages ludicrously disproportionate to the value of his work. We wish, too, they would watch him while, with a hide thicker than that of a hippopotamus, and a body to which fervid heat is a comfort rather than an annoyance, he droningly lounges over the prescribed task on which the intrepid Englishman, uninured to the burning sun, consumes his impatient energy, and too often sacrifices his life. We wish they would go out and view the negro in all the blazonry of his idleness, his pride, his ingratitude, contemptuously sneering at the industry of that race which made him free, and then come home and teach the memorable lesson of their experience to the fanatics who have perverted him into what he is.

* * * * * * * *

The Abolitionists in America would have the population of the Southern States turned into a mixed race, whites, blacks, and mulattoes being on terms of equality, and constantly intermarrying ; but if one thing more than another has tended to give to the Anglo-Saxon race in the New World the victory over the Spanish, it is that it has kept itself apart from the red and negro races, and lodged power constantly in the hands of men of European origin. It has been fully proved, not only on the American continent, but in our own colonies, that the enforced equality of European and African tends, not to the elevation of the black, but the degradation of the white man. We cannot find any sympathy for those who would try, in the United States, the plan of a half-caste Republic, and we trust that the Federal Government and the right-thinking part of the community will protect the South from the repetition of such outrages as that at Harper's Ferry.

Our own race is boastful as well as intolerant and aggressive. This is especially true of the New England type, and hence it is that we are prone to regard ourselves in many, if not all respects, superior to the people of the South. In some respects, undoubtedly, we have the advantage of those who have been born and educated under a very different social system; but, on the other hand, according to the law of compensation, we lack much that is valuable in the Southern character and mental constitution.

The nature of our climate and more especially of our institutions, has given to our English blood a new and most powerful stimulus, so that we develope an immense amount of intellectual energy and activity, which constantly seeks vent, and which constantly tends to run into some extreme or excess. Having lived for many years in a state of great material prosperity, we are prone to wax fat and kick. We have known no real evils, no invasion from without, or civil war within, and for want of any real danger we conjure up those that are imaginary. We torment ourselves with evils which have no existence but in our own brain. I think it was Judge Marshall who speaks of those imaginary evils, which as they are without cause, are also without remedy.

The Southern mind is less active and more conservative, sometimes erratic, but generally disposed to take a common sense and rational view of things, and is, in some respects, more reliable than our own. It forms an admirable check in our political system, and preserves us from a natural tendency to run into the extreme of radicalism, and that spirit of agrarianism which has destroyed all former Republics.

The constant tendency in a Republic is to remove all constitutional checks intended for the security of individual rights, and reduce everything to the rule of the majority. It is obvious that the Senate of the United States and the Supreme Court, though intended as checks upon popular impulse and outbreaks, are yet but very imperfect barriers when opposed to what is termed the will of the people. It requires but a few years to change the political character of the Senate so that it shall reflect the prevailing sentiments of the day, and the same is true of the Supreme Court. In some of our States the judges are already elected from year to year, and must become to a greater or less extent political partizans. When these checks are removed and the rights of the individual are dependant on the bare will of the majority, then we have a pure democracy, which is pure despotism, and a despotism so dreadful that it soon gives way to despotism of a milder form in the person of a military Dictator. We have no landed aristocracy which, in England, stands between the people and the throne, keeping each from encroaching upon the other, nor any real check in our system of government, unless it is the fixed fact of a large number of States, whose population is naturally and necessarily conservative, and which stands like a rock against the surging waves of popular excitement of agrarianism and radicalism from whatever quarter they may come. The assertion that Slavery was the corner-stone of American liberty, made some years ago by a statesman from South Carolina, was looked upon with amazement as a most absurd paradox, but time may show that it contained a truth which we have as yet failed to see and comprehend.

The Southern character is more impulsive, but also more open and genial than our own. If it shows a hasty spark, it is also soon cold and rational again. It is not brooding and intolerant, nor easily led away into excesses, such as too often befall us of a more Northern clime. One prominent cause for such difference is, no doubt, to be found in the fact that, while we, at the North, live in towns and cities where men are in a constant state of action and reaction upon each other, and the masses can be suddenly and extensively roused and excited, the Southern Planters live remote from each other, and, in many cases, in almost entire seclusion. Such a population is less in danger from these moral epidemics that from time to time sweep over communities, because it is sparse, and therefore not so much exposed to exciting causes; thus, while it loses many good influences which flow from a more compact society, escaping also many serious evils to which the latter is subject. It is not France, but Paris, the great centre of population, the seat of all that is luxurious and refined, of science and of art, of everything in short which can serve to adorn and embellish social life; it is this Paris alone that makes and unmakes kings and emperors, that overthrows one dynasty during the night and sets up another the next morning, and then gives the law to the nation which stands looking on. Some editor or some orator touches that sympathetic telegraphic chord which passes through each individual of this vast living mass, and in an instant, as it were, the gutters run with blood, a ferocious mob rushes through every avenue, seeking vengeance for wrongs, which, if they have no existence, in fact, exist not the less really in the excited and inflamed imagination. Then comes a satiety of blood, then a re-action, and then a state of things too often far worse than the first. Our own city of New York is considered by many to have become incapable of intelligent self-government, and to exhibit those evils which, especially under a government like our own, flow from the collection of a very large population at one point. A sparse and widely scattered population, which is also by necessity highly consecutive, may supply the very check we most need and which is not to be found in paper constitutions, courts or senates.

In the gradual progress of time, free labor will doubtless overrun the more Northern Slave States, bringing fertility to the soil, and improving in many respects the condition of the white race, though fraught with ruin to all of African descent. My sympathies are with the latter as well as the former, and I cannot wish to see our swelling, aggressive, Northern Anglo-Saxon tide, over-flowing the Southern States, sweeping away perhaps the most conservative and useful element in our republican system, and at the same time utterly destroying in its course that helpless race which, in the providence of God, has been cast upon our shores. There is room enough for us all to live together in peace and harmony. The two races can co-exist in their present relative condition, but in no other way. This is the great lesson of history, experience, statistics, and the observation of every day.

www.ingramcontent.com/pod-product-compliance
Lightning Source LLC
Chambersburg PA
CBHW020627260626
47157CB00009B/3204